Umty-tiddly, umpty-too
Umty-tiddly, umpty-too
Umty-tiddly, umpty-too
Umty-tiddly, umpty-too
Umty-tiddly, umpty-too
Umty-tiddly, umpty-too
Umty-tiddly, umpty-too
Umty-tiddly, umpty-too
Umty-tiddly, umpty-too

# EGMONT

*We bring stories to life*

This edition published in Great Britain 2008 by Dean
an imprint of Egmont UK Limited
239 Kensington High Street, London W8 6SA
© 2008 Disney Enterprises, Inc
Based on the Winnie-the-Pooh works by A. A. Milne and E. H. Shepard
Illustrations by Andrew Grey
Text by Laura Dollin

ISBN 978 0 6035 6360 7
1 3 5 7 9 10 8 6 4 2
Printed in China

# All About

# Eeyore

This book belongs to . . .

---------------------------------------

# Meet Eeyore

If we were to tell Eeyore that you were here to meet him, he would probably nod gloomily and say, "Really? I'm sure it can't be me you're looking for . . . there must be some mistake." Eeyore is, after all,

## a far-from-merry soul.

You can usually find him standing in a patch of prickly thistles, gazing sadly at the ground, wondering to himself. But all his friends in the Hundred Acre Wood love him very much, and even if he isn't always very good Company, Eeyore appreciates any kindness or friendship that happens to come his way.

# A Poem about Eeyore

Eeyore is old, he's grey and he's slow,
He may, if you're lucky, nod a hello,
But he's probably pondering a sad reflection
And thinking with gloom of his sorry dejection.

Eeyore eats thistles, and wonders "Why?"
He may, if you're lucky, look up with a sigh,
But mostly his low expectations are such
That he's grateful to any who think of him much.

# Facts about Eeyore

🌿 *Eeyore lives in a Rather Gloomy Place by the stream.* It's marshy and muddy and has thistle patches – which he eats, as there's not much else.

🌿 *Eeyore doesn't think very highly of himself.* In fact, he would say it's not really worth writing a book about him. On the other hand he's not sure what *is* worth writing about.

*Eeyore can't swim.* As he discovered when somebody BOUNCED him suddenly from behind, and he had to be helped out of the river.

*Eeyore is very attached to his tail,* but once it came off because Owl thought it was a bell-pull and took it home by mistake.

*Eeyore thinks a lot.* He is often rather grumpy and gloomy, but Eeyore is a sensitive soul. He even, in one of his many Quiet Moments, wrote a poem for Christopher Robin.

*Eeyore can be forgetful.* As well as losing his tail, Eeyore lost his house. But in actual fact, Pooh and Piglet had moved his house to somewhere quite other.

© Disney

*Everything has its uses.* Even a burst balloon and an empty pot can be Useful when you discover, as Eeyore did, that you can put the balloon inside the pot and take it out, over and over again.

# In which we read about

## Eeyore

It was very cold in the Hundred Acre Wood, for it had been

snowing

and

snowing

and

snowing.

It had been snowing so much that Eeyore, who usually lived in Eeyore's Gloomy Place by the stream (so as not to bother anybody), had decided that it was time he had somewhere warmer to live.

So he had slowly
and gloomily
collected some
sticks and then
placed them sadly in
a pile that looked a bit like a house. After that,
he had gone for a melancholy wander to think about
the state of things in the Hundred Acre Wood.

Later that day,
he returned to
where he had
built his house
of sticks to find

that it wasn't there. Miserable and befuddled,
he ambled to Christopher Robin's house.

"Hello, Eeyore!" said Christopher Robin cheerfully when he opened the door.

"It's snowing still," observed Eeyore, gloomily. "And f r e e z i n g cold. And I don't suppose you've seen a house or what-not anywhere about?"

"What sort of a house would that be, Eeyore?"

"My house. At least I thought it was my house as I built it. But the strange thing is, it was there when I left it this morning and when I came back it wasn't. Not at all natural."

"Oh Eeyore, that's terrible," said Christopher Robin. "We must go and look for it at once."

And he went to fetch his coat straight away.

Christopher Robin and Eeyore set off together with Eeyore mumbling about how he couldn't really expect to have a house and he wasn't complaining, but it really wasn't what one could call

Hot at 3 o'clock in the morning these days . . .

Soon they arrived at the corner of the field where Eeyore's house was no longer.

"At least there's some snow left," muttered Eeyore. "I suppose I shouldn't complain."

And at that moment, Christopher Robin hushed him and told him to listen.

In the distance they could hear a deep gruff voice singing about the snow and a small high voice tiddely-pomming in between.

"It's **Pooh** and **Piglet**!" said Christopher Robin excitedly.

"Quite possibly," replied Eeyore. And then the words of the song changed and they heard, *"We've finished our HOUSE!"* followed by *"It's a beautiful HOUSE!"* (with Tiddely-pom in between).

# "Pooh!"

called Christopher Robin and the singing stopped.

"It's Christopher Robin!" they heard Piglet say. "He's round by the place where we got all those sticks from."

The friends rushed to meet each other and when
they had hugged hello, Christopher Robin began
to explain the sad story of Eeyore's Lost House.
As Pooh and Piglet listened, their eyes got
bigger
and
bigger.

"*Where* did you say it was?" asked Pooh.

"Just here," replied Eeyore. "Made of sticks."

"Oh," said Piglet rather nervously, and began to
hum tiddely-pom so as to appear quite at ease.

"What's the matter?" said Christopher Robin.

"Well," began Pooh. "The fact *is*," said Pooh.

"The fact is, you see ..." said Pooh. "Well,
we thought it might be warmer at the other
side of the wood."

"Warmer for what?" asked Christopher Robin.

"For Eeyore's house," said Pooh firmly.

Eeyore tried to say that his house had been *here*, but
before he could mumble very much, Pooh and Piglet
had led him round
the corner.
And there was
Eeyore's
house, looking
as comfy as
anything.

"It has an Inside as well as an Outside," explained Pooh proudly.

And just to make sure, Eeyore went inside . . . and came out again.

"Quite remarkable," he said at last. "The wind must have blown it here. And somehow it got better on the way."

"Much better,"

said Pooh and Piglet together.

And with that, leaving Eeyore in his house,
Pooh and Piglet took Christopher Robin
back for lunch and, on the way, told him of the
Awful Mistake they had made.

Luckily, Christopher Robin laughed a lot.

A few weeks later, when the snow had disappeared and he was well and truly settled in his new house, Eeyore was plodding slowly down the stream when Winnie-the-Pooh appeared.

"Good morning, Eeyore!"

said Pooh, cheerfully.

"Good morning, Pooh Bear," replied Eeyore gloomily. "If it is a good morning," he added.

"Oh dear, what's the matter?" said Pooh.

Eeyore explained that there was nothing, absolutely nothing, not even a tiny thing the matter, and that he really wasn't complaining, for it couldn't matter less, and that he really shouldn't be sad on his birthday which, after all, was the happiest day of the year . . .

"Your *birthday*?" said Pooh in surprise.

Eeyore said that of course it was his birthday and couldn't Pooh see all the presents lying around and the birthday cake with candles and pink icing?

Pooh was rather puzzled, for he couldn't see any presents at all. Or, for that matter, any cake with candles and pink icing.

"I can't see any of those things," he said.

And Eeyore grunted miserably and agreed he couldn't see them either, ha ha.

Pooh scratched his head and wished Eeyore many happy returns of the day anyway.

Then, leaving Eeyore to mutter
about nobody taking any notice of his birthday,
Pooh hurried home as quickly as he could.
He felt very sad about Eeyore
and wanted to find him a present.

Outside Pooh's house,
Piglet was jumping
up
 and
 down,
trying to reach
the knocker.

MR SAUDERS

"Hello, Pooh!" said Piglet.

"I was just coming to see you . . ."

"I've just seen Eeyore," interrupted Pooh.
"And he's in a Very Sad Condition because it's
his birthday and nobody has taken any notice.
He's very Gloomy indeed.
We must take him a present."

The two friends went inside Pooh's house and Pooh
went straight to his honey cupboard to see what he
could find. He had lots of honey pots but only one
with any honey left inside!

"I'm going to
give this to Eeyore,"
he said proudly.

Piglet thought for
a moment and then
he remembered that
he had one
balloon left from
his party and would
go and get it to
cheer up Eeyore.

And so Pooh set off with his jar of honey and Piglet trotted home to fetch the balloon.

It was a warm day, and Pooh began to get a *funny* feeling creeping over him, from the tip of his nose, right down to the end of his toes.

He knew that feeling. It was a feeling that told him that it was time for a **little something**.

And, with that, he sat down and took the lid off
his jar of honey.

He began to eat,
and eat ...
and
eat.

And as he licked the last drop of honey, he
wondered where it was he had been going.

"Ah, yes, Eeyore!" he said. And then "Bother!"
when he realised he'd eaten Eeyore's birthday
present. *What could he give him instead?* He
thought for a while and then decided that the pot
was a very nice pot even without the honey inside,
and surely Eeyore might find it Useful.

Pooh continued on his way, and as he was passing
Owl's house in the Wood he called in to see him.
Showing Owl his Useful Pot for Eeyore, Owl said
that he should write "*A Happy Birthday*" on it.
Pooh thought that was a very good idea and asked
Owl to help him.

Which he did, nodding wisely as he wrote:

HIPY PAPY BTHUTHDTH THUTHDA BTHUTHDY.

("A Very Happy Birthday with love from Pooh.")

Meanwhile, Piglet had
fetched his balloon and was
holding on to it very **tightly**
so that it wouldn't blow away.

He *ran* as fast as he could,
so that he might get to Eeyore before Pooh, and
thinking just how pleased Eeyore was going to be,
he forgot to look where he was going.

His foot landed in a rabbit hole and he fell
flat on his face:  B A N G ! ! ! !

For a moment, Piglet wondered what
could have happened.
Had the Forest fallen down?
Or had he blown up?
Perhaps he was far away on the moon . . . then he looked
down and realised that it was *he* who had fallen down and
that his poor balloon had popped and
was now nothing more than
a small piece of rag.

"Oh dear!" said Piglet.
"Oh dear, oh dear,
oh dearie dearie dear."
Now his present for Eeyore wasn't such a good one.
Never mind, perhaps Eeyore didn't like balloons so very
much anyway? He would still take it to him, so he trotted
on sadly to the stream where Eeyore was.

Eeyore was just gazing at his reflection in the water, concluding that it was a very sorry sight, when he heard Piglet's voice behind him.

"Good morning, Eeyore!" said Piglet. "And many happy returns of the day!"

Eeyore turned around gloomily and stared at Piglet. "I've brought you a present!" continued Piglet, excitedly. "It's a balloon!"

Eeyore could feel his gloom slipping away. Now he was getting a balloon it really did feel like a birthday.

"But Eeyore," continued Piglet.
"I'm SO sorry,

      SO very,

            very sorry,

I'm afraid when I was bringing it to you I fell

over and I

       - BURST -

                      the balloon."

There was a long silence.

"*My* balloon?" said Eeyore
at last, and Piglet nodded. He held
out the little piece of damp rag.
Eeyore looked at it and Piglet felt
really rather miserable.

But Eeyore didn't seem too upset and asked Piglet
what colour it had been when it *was* a balloon. When
Piglet told him that it had been red, Eeyore said, "Thank
you, Piglet. My *favourite* colour."

Just then, Winnie-the-Pooh arrived.

"Happy Birthday, Eeyore!" he called.

"I've brought you
a present too."
He gave Eeyore the
Useful Pot
and Eeyore became
quite excited.

"Look, little Piglet!"
Eeyore exclaimed.
"I do believe that the balloon you gave me will fit very
nicely into this rather Useful pot!"

Piglet looked on hopefully as Eeyore
put the balloon in the pot.

**"There you are!"** said Eeyore.

And Pooh and Piglet were very happy indeed
that Eeyore was so pleased with his presents.

In fact, when it came to say

goodbye

and

Happy Birthday

once again, Eeyore hardly
noticed that his friends were going, for he was
*far* too busy taking the balloon

**out** and

putting it **back** in again,

happy as can be.

What a perfect present!

Umty-tiddly, umpty-too

Umty-tiddly, umpty-too

Umty-tiddly, umpty-too

Umty-tiddly, umpty-too

Umty-tiddly, umpty-too

Umty-tiddly, umpty-too

Umty-tiddly, umpty-too

Umty-tiddly, umpty-too

Umty-tiddly, umpty-too

Umty-tiddly, umpty-too
Umty-tiddly, umpty-too
Umty-tiddly, umpty-too
Umty-tiddly, umpty-too
Umty-tiddly, umpty-
Umty-tiddly, umpty-too
Umty-tiddly, umpty-too
Umty-tiddly, umpty-too
Umty-tiddly, umpty-t
Umty-tiddly, umpty-too
Umty-tiddly, umpty-too